A Tragedy *at the* Theatre

The Lady Jane & Mrs Forbes Mysteries
A Novella

B. D. CHURSTON

ABOUT THIS NOVELLA

"A Tragedy at the Theatre" is a novella-length tale from the Lady Jane and Mrs Forbes series of light-hearted, 1920s historical cozy mysteries. It's a stand-alone story that can be enjoyed at any point in the series but, chronologically, it sits between the first and second novels.

Of course, we understand that a stand-alone novella might not be picked up by everyone. To avoid confusion, Kate and Jane's sleuthing in 'A Tragedy at the Theatre' is not referred to in any of the full-length novels.

One

Kate Forbes was more than a little excited by the whole business. As a widow living alone, it was rare these days to be doing something unexpected.

Her niece, Lady Jane Scott, and a friend called Lottie had planned a trip to the Astoria Theatre in Southshore – only for Lottie to go down with a heavy cold, leaving Jane without a companion.

With 'Spring Cleaning' the sole item on Kate's to-do list, it had been a fairly trouble-free decision to abandon her house and replace Jane's unfortunate pal.

On that basis, Lottie's hotel room was quickly reassigned, a hefty travel bag packed, and a morning train taken from Kate's home in Sandham-on-Sea to Southshore, ten miles along the coast.

At Southshore station, Kate met up with Jane, who had come direct from London. A convivial lunch at their hotel followed and here they were – on a Friday afternoon under a brooding sky – wearing raincoats and making their way on foot to the nearby Astoria.

Despite the showery weather, Kate was in a joyous mood. This was no common or lesser-spotted theatre trip – this was one as guests of a member of the company. As a result, not only had Jane secured excellent seats for that evening's performance of J. M. Barrie's *The Admirable Crichton*, they would also be fussed over that afternoon with a guided tour of the theatre and permission to watch rehearsals for next week's play, the Arnold Bennett comedy, *The Honeymoon*.

"Do you think we'll be called into action during rehearsals?" Kate wondered as they neared the theatre.

Jane was taken aback.

"On the stage, Aunt?"

"No, I mean will they expect us to laugh as if it were the opening night – albeit with only two audience members."

"Well…"

"It's a worry, isn't it. What if I don't laugh when I'm meant to. Or worse…"

"Worse?"

"Yes, what if uncertainty takes over and I laugh at parts that aren't meant to be funny. They might think there's something wrong with me."

"Yes… well… I expect we'll be asked to keep quiet."

Kate glanced at her niece. The warm brown eyes and friendly smile… the short brown hair tucked behind the ears… the sharp, meticulous mind – she was an impressive, kind-hearted young woman.

A few minutes later, they came to a halt by a parade of shops on King Alfred Street opposite the theatre.

"The Astoria, Aunt. We're expected at the stage door."

"Wonderful."

They paused to take in the Victorian frontage with its posters for *The Admirable Crichton* on notice boards either side of half-glass doors leading to the foyer, box office, stalls and circle. Kate thought the place looked a little tired but kept it to herself.

"So… the stage door…?" she said, peering into a downward sloping alley running along the right-hand side of the theatre. Here, large double doors into the building had ground shutters in front – those that would be lifted open to take beer barrels to the cellar. Would this also serve as the stage door? Not that they would be able to get that far – the wrought iron gates across the top of the alley were closed.

"It's on the other side of the building, Aunt."

"Ah…"

They crossed King Alfred Street and headed into Little Alfred Street, which separated the theatre on one side from the high wall of a timber supplies firm on the other.

Kate disliked the side street's dank, narrow character and the way it sloped down to a dead end at the foot of another high wall, over which appeared to be a chemical factory.

However, approaching a side door into the theatre a few yards down, her mood soared.

"Just think, Jane – countless famous actors must have passed through this very entrance ready to throw off their ordinary clothing to entertain those within."

The door had a sign: 'OFFICE'.

"Ah… then again…"

"Aunt?" said Jane, pointing to more doors farther down the slope.

They duly followed in the footsteps of Kate's imagined actors past a couple of rusty metal dustbins outside the 'GENERAL DELIVERIES' double doors and around a couple of muddy puddles to arrive at the farthest side entrance.

Here, the sign was more helpful: 'STAGE DOOR'.

"Ah… the portal to a world of glitz and glamour," Kate mused, although the chipped and faded paintwork had her wondering.

Two

As they entered an unattractive vestibule, a faint whiff of damp assailed Kate's nostrils. She supposed that the downward slope of the street outside meant they were now below the level the public would be familiar with inside the building. A vast gloomy basement, no less.

For Kate, its dullness wasn't helped by scuffed off-white plastered walls and time-worn bare floorboards. Clearly, presentations on the stage were at odds with life behind the scenery. Then again, she supposed there wasn't the revenue here that the London theatres commanded.

"Hey! Hello! Welcome to the Astoria!"

They turned to the source of the cheery greeting – a vibrant young woman with fair hair tied in a ponytail. She looked relaxed in an old sapphire blouse and a functional knee-length grey skirt.

"Hetty!" declared Jane. "How are you?"

The introductions followed and Kate now had a welcoming face to put with the knowledge Jane had imparted earlier – that the Honourable Henrietta 'Hetty' Bryce was a twenty-three-year-old cousin on Jane's father's side. Apparently, parental approval of Hetty's foray into the world of acting was yet to be forthcoming.

"Let's pop those coats in my dressing room, shall we."

Removing their outer garments, a clammy Kate was happy to be down to her dark emerald day dress and matching cardigan, while Jane looked freer in a deep crimson two-piece.

Handing their coats to Hetty, they set off along the corridor leading across the back of the building.

"We have eight dressing rooms," said Hetty, referring to a line of doors that stretched ahead on their left. "Hugh first, then Carole, empty, empty, Richard, Spencer, me, and Angela. You'll get to meet everyone soon enough."

"Right," said Kate, trying to remember all the names.

"What have you been up to, Jane?" Hetty asked. "Dusty documents or muddy trenches?"

"Dusty documents. I won't be digging for a while yet."

"Hmm, you'll also have other things in mind now that the vapid Viscount's out of the way."

Kate might have cringed. It was one thing to ask about historical and archaeological pursuits, but another entirely to refer to Jane ending her engagement. However, these two were cousins and friends. Indeed, Jane was smiling.

"We'll see. How about you?"

"Me? I'm married to the Astoria, Jane."

It had already been arranged that Hetty would show them around the theatre, and Kate was ready to get started despite the drabness of the corridors.

"Don't worry," said Hetty, seemingly reading Kate's mind, "they do spend a bit of money on the old place when it's essential."

"Oh no, Hetty, I was merely thinking the Astoria has an abundance of... character."

"To be honest, Mrs Forbes, it's a perennial fight to make money. In recent years, the Astoria has been battling with a couple of moving picture houses for audiences."

Kate was sympathetic but had no advice to offer. People enjoyed watching films. She did so herself – most recently, two evenings ago, although it had been annoying to have the man sitting behind her reading out every caption on the screen. So much for *silent* movies.

"The theatre-goers club is a help," said Hetty. "Members tend to book ahead in fair numbers."

"It's all about offering the right plays then," said Jane.

"Yes and no. They love a good melodrama, but our director insists they take regular doses of serious theatre."

"That's where comfy seats come into it," said Kate. "I once had a hard wooden pew for a four-hour performance of *Coriolanus*."

She omitted saying that it caused such numbness in a certain quarter that she couldn't have cared less what happened in the final act.

Hetty's dressing room was the second from last. Here, Kate and Jane remained at the doorway while Hetty entered and hung their coats on a free-standing rack.

"No surprises here," she said. "Our dressing rooms aren't very glamorous, but they give us somewhere to get ready and go over our lines without interruption."

The plain room was indeed lacking in charm. Even its window opened onto a bleak back alley with a facing high wall blocking out much of the light.

"A safe haven," said Kate cheerfully.

She noticed part of her reflection in a narrow full-length mirror on a wooden stand beside the dressing table and so shuffled sideways a little for a proper look. The grey strands in her hair weren't about to vanish but the extra walking she'd recently undertaken was beginning to have a slight effect.

"It should hopefully be an interesting day for you," said Hetty as she re-emerged. "We'll just collect Richard and then it's on with the guided tour."

"It's so kind," said Kate. "Are you sure we're not putting you out?"

"Not at all. It's customary to give special guests a proper look around. Besides, it's no secret that our director, Neville Calder, likes to put visitors in a receptive frame of mind before trapping them into becoming sponsors."

"Oh… right… I see," said Kate, somewhat alarmed at the prospect.

"Now, let's collect Richard," said Hetty.

Heading back the way they came, they passed the next door along – with Hetty reminding them that it belonged to Spencer – and knocked on the one after.

Kate meanwhile turned to Jane and whispered.

"They're after our money."

Jane whispered back at her.

"Sorry about that, Aunt. It was all so last-minute, I forgot to mention it. Just leave Neville Calder to me."

Kate attempted a smile. Despite the prospect of having her purse raided, it was time to focus on the positive aspects of their visit.

"I'm looking forward to this," she said brightly. "I've seen many theatrical productions, but I've never attended a professional company's rehearsals before."

"Me neither," said Jane. "It should be fun."

Three

Hetty's fellow tour guide joined them — a tall, casually-dressed chap of around thirty with a wave of mousy brown hair over an expressive, friendly face. Introductions revealed him to be Richard Harding, an aspiring actor and playwright who had been with the company for a couple of years.

"I'm also studying under Neville Calder to become a director," said Richard. "I usually lead the first day or two of rehearsals to get us reasonably ship-shape before Neville takes over."

"That's quite a bit of juggling if you're in the scene you're directing," Kate surmised.

"Yes, but fun too."

"Good for you," said Kate, enjoying his enthusiasm.

"Now, let's get going," said Hetty. "It's time to take you to the heart of the Astoria — the stage."

Both Kate and Jane beamed.

"It's set for tonight's performance," said Richard. "You can try it out if you like."

"Are you sure?" Kate was delighted. "I won't act, of course."

Hetty smiled. "If the urge takes you – you must!"

The idea gave Kate butterflies.

"We'll take the longer way round so you get to see the storage area where we keep our spare scenery and props," said Richard.

"Wonderful," said Kate.

She was already thoroughly enjoying the tour – and they had yet to go anywhere.

"This way," said Richard, taking them back towards the stage door. "While our dressing rooms are hardly special, there is an exception. Hugh Calder is the Astoria's owner and principal player, so…"

He was pointing to the room nearest the stage door.

"I'm guessing Hugh's dressing room isn't plain," said Kate.

"No, it's much grander and three times the size of the others," gushed Hetty. "It originally belonged to their grandmother, Nora Calder. She was a fine actress, by all accounts."

"Are Hugh and Neville brothers?" asked Kate.

"Yes, Hugh's the eldest of three. The youngest brother, Stephen, lives in New York. He's dedicated himself to the investment business, sensible chap."

Just then, the door to Hugh's dressing room opened and two people appeared. One was a lean man of around fifty, with thinning grey hair, steel blue eyes and a firm jaw.

The woman with him was much younger, possibly in her late twenties, with a round, friendly face, and long black hair tied into plaits.

"Ah!" said Richard. "How timely."

"Visitors?" boomed Hugh, his voice filling the entire space and no doubt echoing far beyond.

Richard turned to the guests.

"May I introduce Mr Hugh Calder and Miss Carole Adams." He then turned to Hugh and Carole. "Mrs Kate Forbes and her niece, Lady Jane Scott are having a guided tour before rehearsals."

"Marvellous!" declared Hugh. "A pleasure to meet you, ladies." He bowed slightly. "Do enjoy your time in our humble home."

Hugh headed off while Carole flashed them an uneasy smile before entering the next dressing room along and closing the door.

"This way," said Hetty, leading them away.

Kate had no intention of putting her nose where it didn't belong, but there seemed to be an element of awkwardness about whatever arrangement there might be between Hugh and Carole.

"Hugh's helping Carole improve her stage presence," said Richard self-consciously. "She's very talented, but there's no harm in striving to become even better."

"It must be quite something to be a principal player," said Jane.

"Yes, Hugh takes great pride in his work," said Hetty before lowering her voice conspiratorially. "It's a well-known secret that he's been almost forty for the past ten years." She raised her voice again. "He's very much admired for his talent and vast experience. There's no finer leading man."

"Unfortunately, not all admiration is healthy," said Richard. "Poor Hugh has an unwanted admirer at the moment. One who's turned poison and started sending him rotten letters."

Kate's eyes widened.

"Threatening letters?"

"I'm not sure. None of us has actually set eyes on them."

Jane frowned.

"Has he told the police?"

"He has," said Hetty, "but apparently the letters are anonymous. I don't think there's much they can do."

"The police have other priorities," said Richard matter-of-factly. "I'm sure it'll stop eventually. These people must get bored after a time."

"Poison pen letters though…" said Kate. It made her shudder.

"It's a pity the police aren't interested," said Jane. "A little effort might narrow it down to someone he met not too long ago."

"Ah…" said Hetty. "The thing is, Hugh meets lots of admirers. Especially women."

"I see," said Jane. "So, the police are probably right. Narrowing it down might be difficult."

Just ahead, a middle-aged woman with a tired demeanour was approaching.

"Guests?" she asked.

The introductions were the usual affair but the bit that leapt out for Kate was Richard saying, "This is Angela Calder, Hugh's wife."

"Thank you for coming," said Angela, beaming at Kate and Jane. "We love having visitors take an interest."

"Thanks for having us," said Jane.

"Absolutely," echoed Kate.

"You'll find lots of lovely people at the Astoria."

"Yes, we've just met your husband."

"It's a lovely old place," said Angela, somewhat abruptly. "I'm never happier than when I'm on stage here performing for the public. Are you staying for rehearsals?"

"Yes," said Kate. "We're looking forward to it."

"Wonderful. You'll get to see some of the hard work that goes into a production. I'm still not happy with some aspects of next week's play, but you'll be able to watch us iron them out."

"It's a privilege," said Kate. "We certainly won't get in the way."

Angela wished them well and continued on her way.

It left Kate wondering. Just how harmonious were productions at the Astoria? It wasn't lost on her that Angela might suspect her husband of having an affair with Carole Adams. It wouldn't have escaped the notice of the rest of the cast either.

"I believe we were heading for the stage," said Richard. "Rehearsals begin in twenty minutes. Let's have it to ourselves for a bit."

Kate brightened and nodded eagerly.

"Lead on, Macduff!"

Four

As promised, their route took them past the props storage area. While there was a clear path to the 'General Deliveries' double doors that opened onto Little Alfred Street, one side of the space housed chock-full shelving, while the opposite wall was home to an array of larger items.

Here they marvelled at the objects awaiting a turn on the stage – from small decorative lamps, sparkly trinket boxes, and exotic ornaments on one side… to a bulky sailor's chest, a white wooden rocking horse, and a fully-decorated Christmas tree on the other.

A thought struck Kate.

"For some reason, I'm imagining a play where all of this is on the stage."

Hetty laughed.

"Now that would be quite the production!"

"Speaking of the stage…" said Richard.

They were soon heading farther down the corridor, although they turned left quite quickly to face two short flights of steps – one going up and one down.

"Downstairs is a space beneath the stage," Richard explained. "There are two trap doors in the stage floor to get access to anything stored there."

"It's also useful for magicians who wish to make someone disappear," said Hetty with a wink.

Richard indicated that they should take the upward flight to the edge of the theatre's focal point.

"You probably know this," he said, "but either side of the stage, out of the audience's view, are the wings. We're stage right… that is, it's to the right of the actor as they face the audience."

On the stage itself, a wonderful Victorian era drawing room had been set out, with a fireplace, comfortable-looking armchairs and other stylish furnishings – nicely ready for the evening performance.

"Ahem," said Hetty. "Enter Mrs Forbes, stage right."

The thrill of it grabbed Kate's heart.

"Are you sure?" she asked.

"Yes," said Richard. "It's time to make your entrance, Mrs Forbes."

"Oh… alright…"

Preparing to step onto the stage, Kate imagined an expectant audience. That terrified her though, so she settled for the hall being empty.

"Right… here goes…"

Surprisingly, there *was* an audience – of one man barging through the doors at the back of the stalls and stopping to stare.

"That's Bill, our caretaker-handyman," said Hetty, having entered the stage behind Kate. "He's a good sort. Without him, we wouldn't get very far. In fact, there are quite a few others we rely on – a wardrobe mistress who's currently working on costumes at home, and our box office ladies and barmaids who come in later."

"Why not have a bit of fun, Mrs Forbes?" suggested Richard. "Is there a recital you'd like to deliver?"

"A… recital…?" Kate swallowed drily.

Feeling self-conscious, she was pleased to note that neither Jane, Richard nor Hetty seemed to see anything unusual in someone acting while on a stage.

"I know a few lines from *A Midsummer Night's Dream*. I was Helena in a school production."

Richard beamed.

"That most loyal of characters!"

"Go on," said Hetty.

"Your time has come, Aunt," said Jane.

Kate cast her mind back to the exact words from Act One before clearing her throat. She then wondered if her voice would function properly. What if she sounded like a laryngitic hippopotamus?

"Love looks not with the eyes, but with the mind, and therefore is winged Cupid painted blind."

She felt daft.

"Enough Shakespeare," she declared. "Who would spend their money to see me on the stage?"

Jane smiled.

"To pay or not to pay. That is the question."

Kate couldn't help but smile too.

"Yes, Jane, whether it is nobler to throw rotten tomatoes or not."

She eyed Bill the caretaker-handyman waiting in the aisle.

"A neutral observer," she said. "Bill? What's your verdict on my performance?"

"With respect, madam, I'd say get off."

"Really? That seems a bit harsh…?"

"I have to check the flats."

"The flats…?"

Richard explained that the flats were the covered timber frames providing the backdrop scenery – in this case, a posh Victorian drawing room complete with a functioning door.

"So, my time hasn't come after all," Kate lamented with a wink to Jane.

Hetty rescued her.

"Let's head up to the circle. The upstairs bar has some interesting architectural features."

A few moments later, they pushed through the doors at the back of the stalls into the foyer. This was a vast, brightly painted area with a box office counter off to their right, behind which a door was marked 'OFFICE.'

Before they set foot on the stairs up to the circle though, voices could be heard from somewhere above.

"I wish you wouldn't listen to gossip, Spencer. It's beneath you."

"I can hardly escape it. It's completely embarrassing."

Kate knew right away that this was Carole Adams. Spencer, she didn't know.

"You're overreacting," said Carole.

"Oh really?"

Spencer seemed ready to argue the point, so Kate opted for a distraction.

"Richard, do you find it odd rehearsing for one play while standing on a set for another?"

Richard smiled bravely as he halted their progress.

"Um... no, you get used to it. Er... let's pay a visit to the office first, shall we?"

"Spencer Wetherby," said Hetty *sotto voce*. "He and Carole are quite close."

"Ah, right," said Kate, unsure what to make of it. At the Astoria, there seemed to be as much drama off the stage as on it.

It caused her to ponder. If passions were running high between Hugh and Carole, then both Angela and Spencer would be having a challenging time of it right now.

"Neville Calder runs the place," Hetty informed them as they neared the office. "He's like a father figure to all of us. A *grumpy* father figure, but he has a real passion for theatre."

At the office door though, it wasn't Neville they could hear, but his brother, Hugh.

"Just trust in me, brother. Come the summer, we'll have packed houses. You'll see I'm right."

"You're driving me mad," seethed Neville. "It has to stop!"

"No, I'll tell you what has to stop – you taking money from visitors when it's not necessary!"

While Kate grappled with Hugh's over-confidence that his quality would pull in the crowds, Richard knocked and pushed the door open.

"I've brought our visitors."

"Ah, splendid," said Neville, instantly transforming his mood. "Do come in."

Hugh was sitting on the edge of a whitewashed desk on one side of the office. He smiled but left without a word, leaving them to his brother – a grey-haired man with a thin black moustache and tired grey eyes. He was sitting behind a sturdy oak desk on the other side of the room.

Hetty turned to the guests.

"Mrs Forbes, Lady Jane... our director, Neville Calder."

"A pleasure to meet you both," said Neville. "Please take a seat. Lady Jane, I understand your father is the Earl of Oxley."

"Yes, that's right."

"How fascinating. You'll have to excuse my ignorance, but where is the family seat?"

"Oxley House is in Northamptonshire."

"Ah, not in the south then."

"No, although my father spends most of his time at the family residence in Mayfair, London – as do I."

"And do either yourself or your father have a passion for theatre?"

Five

The tour guides steered the beleaguered visitors out of the office and into the foyer.

"The Grand Circle next," said Hetty, seemingly keen to rescue them as quickly as possible from Neville Calder's charm offensive, which had netted a far-too-generous contribution from Jane – although Jane had presented it as a joint gift from herself and her aunt.

At the top of the stairs, they entered a vast lounge area with a bar on one side. Here, over the long years, the whiff of stale beer had bonded with the fabric of the building.

"Our audiences enjoy *most* of our performances," said Hetty. "If they don't… we have the downstairs and upstairs bars."

"We've seen it many a time," said Richard, leading them across the expanse towards the grand circle bar. "Certain patrons finding the play not to their taste, but following it with several drinks, after which they roll outside telling everyone what a great night they've had."

"I'm sure Neville Calder would approve," said Kate, peering out of a window that overlooked the alley by the beer cellar doors below.

"He sometimes serves the drinks himself," said Hetty, "to help drive up profits. There's a history of it in the family."

"Oh?" said Kate.

Richard glanced left and right, as if making sure they wouldn't be overheard.

"Around the turn of the century, Hugh and Neville's father, Ewan Calder, was a ferocious champion for serious theatre. He thought nothing of boosting shrinking profits with booze – often a little too enthusiastically though. He ended up in court charged with keeping the bars open till midnight and allowing raucous behaviour."

"He incurred a hefty fine," said Hetty, "which wiped out the beer profits to such a degree that he had to do it again to make up the shortfall."

Kate smiled at the cheek of it.

"There *was* a golden age," said Richard. "Around the 1880s and 1890s, John Campbell Calder, the founder, seemed to find just the blend – mainly music hall type entertainment on Fridays and Saturdays, with light drama during the week. It didn't last though – his son, Ewan Calder took over."

"They keep it in the family then," Kate observed.

"Yes, Hugh and Neville are the third generation."

Kate admired the family's passion for the theatre down the years. As for Hetty and Richard – perhaps a bright future of their own awaited. They certainly seemed to get along, although that was none of her business, of course.

"Let's take in the view of the stage from the grand circle, shall we?" said Richard.

"Lovely," said Kate. "That's where we'll be sitting for tonight's performance."

They pushed through some doors onto the sweeping arc of the upper level. These seats gave a wonderfully clear view of the whole of the stage, including its depth.

"Oh, I do love a seat at the front of the circle," Kate enthused.

She tried to imagine watching her own brief foray into Shakespeare from here but entering from stage right was a wailing Carole Adams.

"I wonder what that's all about?" said Hetty.

"Are you alright?" Richard called down.

Carole looked up but could only wail further. This made up their minds to hurry downstairs.

Moments later, they met with a tear-streaked Carole at the front of the stage.

"Hugh…" she cried.

"What about him?" said a worried Kate.

"Someone shot him…" was all she could add.

"Goodness me!" Kate exclaimed.

"I'll get Neville to call the police," said Richard already racing off towards the office.

"Where's Hugh?" Hetty asked Carole.

"In his dressing room."

"I'd better take a look," said Hetty.

Kate flashed a glance at Jane, which she hoped conveyed an intention to not let Hetty go alone.

Jane nodded and they were quickly behind the young actress.

"I'm sure Carole's wrong," was Hetty's only comment.

It didn't take long to arrive at Hugh's dressing room where the door was slightly ajar.

Somewhat fearfully, Kate pushed it open.

"Oh my," she gasped.

Inside, the company's principal actor was slumped forward over his dressing table with what appeared to be a gunshot wound in the middle of his back.

She pulled the door closed.

"We'll wait for the police."

Six

Neville and Richard met Sergeant Halstead and Constable Shanks at the main entrance and without delay led them through the foyer, across the stalls, up onto the stage and down into the corridor that led to Hugh's dressing room.

Kate, Jane and a fearful gaggle of company folk were waiting outside. Among them, a red-eyed Angela looked set to break down.

Without a word, Sergeant Halstead entered the dressing room while the constable took up a position beside the door.

A few moments later, the sergeant came outside again.

"Who found Mr Calder?"

"I did," said Carole.

"Did you disturb anything?"

"No, I… went to find help."

"Hmm… did anyone hear a gunshot?"

A murmured consensus conveyed that no-one had, which caused the sergeant to wrinkle his nose.

"A small-bore weapon then. Behind a closed door… and I'm assuming the rest of you were busy elsewhere?"

"Yes," said Spencer.

"The weapon's not there then?" Hetty surmised.

"I'm not here to answer questions," Sergeant Halstead advised.

Kate studied Hetty. Despite putting a brave face on it, the young actress would be suffering. Kate certainly was, despite this being her second experience of the dreaded act.

"Did Mr Calder have any enemies?" asked the sergeant.

"Apparently so," said Angela, her voice quivering.

Halstead closed his eyes for a moment before refining his inquiry.

"I appreciate how difficult this must be, but did he have any enemies among the people in this building?"

"Of course not," insisted Spencer.

"Then… did Mr Calder have any enemies more generally. And would anyone be able to name one for me?"

"I can't give you a name," said Carole, "but Hugh told me he was receiving horrible anonymous letters."

"Like this one?"

The sergeant held up a sheet of paper with words cut from a newspaper glued to it.

"I expect so," said Carole. "Hugh was giving me acting guidance. He never showed me any of them."

Kate tried to read it, but Halstead lowered his hand with the words facing inward.

"My brother mentioned the letters to me too," said a pale Neville. "I believe he'd been receiving them for the past couple of weeks or so. I never realised it was so serious."

"If the assailant were an outsider, there were some footprints," said Jane, "although we appear to have trodden all over them."

"They look quite muddy," said Neville. "That is, what's left of them…"

"Possibly a woman's shoe," said the constable. "Then again…"

The sergeant looked down at his large boots, which confirmed his part in the disturbance. He then held aloft the evidence in his hand once more, which *once more* Kate tried and failed to read.

"This was on his dressing table. As it's the only one in there, I'd say it was left by the assailant."

"I think you'll find the others at the police station," said Carole.

"Ah… that would seem to confirm it then. Who else knew of the letters?"

While Angela nodded, Spencer remained impassive, which Kate wondered about. His girlfriend was no longer under the spell of the senior man.

"Hugh's trouble with an admirer was generally known," said Richard. "It's the first I've seen of the letters though."

"Hugh was a changed man," said Carole. "In the past, he'd invite admirers to his dressing room. But he'd recently put all that behind him."

"And yet, you were spending time in there with him," Angela sniffled.

"Everyone knows it was perfectly innocent," Carole insisted.

"Innocent? I'd call it intense."

"Yes… but only because Hugh was pushing me to learn quickly."

"Alright, alright," said Sergeant Halstead, looking to reduce the heat of the moment.

Kate looked to see what Jane made of it. Typically, her niece seemed absorbed by everything being said.

"I can't take any more," said Angela, turning away and shuffling off. The indistinct words trailing behind her suggested that, if needed, she would be in her dressing room.

"I'm wondering how the perpetrator got in," said the sergeant.

"Bill, our caretaker is always first in," said Hetty. "He has a key for the main door. He unbolts the stage door half an hour before rehearsals."

All looked in that direction.

"The stage door wasn't locked then," Halstead observed.

"It has no lock," said Neville. "In the event of a fire, it serves as an escape route."

Kate eyed the hefty top and bottom bolts. When closed, they would secure the door but also prevent anyone being locked in during an emergency.

"How long does it remain open?" the sergeant asked.

"During rehearsals?" contemplated Neville. "It's bolted shut by the last to leave for the stage. That's almost always Hugh."

"So… the assailant most likely got in by the stage door… came along to the dressing room… no weapon left behind. Is it possible they got out another way?"

"I was in the far corridor," said Spencer. "I like to walk where it's quiet before I go to the stage for rehearsals. No one came by."

"What *far* corridor?"

The sergeant sounded weary, but Spencer shrugged as if it were common knowledge.

"On the other side of the building. If you go far enough, it leads to the cellar beneath the stalls bar."

"But no one came that way?"

"No. Mind you, they wouldn't have got far. The cellar door was bolted shut."

Halstead turned to look elsewhere for inspiration.

"Mrs Calder?" he called out.

Some distance away, Angela had just reached her door but was yet to enter. She turned slowly, tiredly.

"Mrs Calder, did you see or hear *anything*?"

"I was in here," she called back with some irritation. She was pointing into her room.

"And you're sure you didn't hear a gunshot?"

She thought for a moment.

"If I did, I didn't know it. There are so many odd noises in a theatre."

If the sergeant had another question, his chance vanished with Angela's entry into her room and the sound of the door closing firmly behind her.

The constable piped up.

"Should I get a list of women the victim saw in his dressing room?"

"Don't be daft, Shanks." Sergeant Halstead then relented. "I don't suppose anyone knows of any visitors, including friendly ones, over the past few months?"

"Not names, Sergeant," said Richard. "Sorry."

Halstead sniffed slightly.

"Alright then, one last time. Wherever you were, did any of you see or hear *anything* or *anyone*?"

"I was at the back of the stalls," said Carole. "I didn't see anyone. Then I went to ask Hugh about something…"

"I was in the office with the inner door open," said Neville. "It gives a view of the foyer, but I don't think anyone came through."

"I didn't see anything," said Hetty. "Richard and I were just finishing showing Mrs Forbes and Lady Jane around before rehearsals got under way. We were in the circle when we heard Carole."

Bill the caretaker-handyman had been standing quietly behind everyone. It was now his time to speak.

"I did a few checks on the scenery. Then I was in the downstairs bar fixing a rickety stool. I didn't see anyone."

"So, the rest of you were soon all to gather for rehearsals," said Halstead.

"Well," huffed Spencer, "we'd have gathered and then waited for Hugh. He was always last. Something to do with his star status."

The sergeant puffed out his cheeks.

"That settles it then. The killer most likely escaped the way they came in – via the stage door. Now, I'd like you all to go and sit somewhere… the front seats by the stage might be best. While Constable Shanks takes some details, I just need to check a couple of things."

"Will tonight's performance be cancelled?" asked the constable. He was looking uncertainly from Sergeant Halstead to Neville Calder and back.

Both answered in the affirmative.

"Might you call in Scotland Yard?" said Kate.

This time, it was only the sergeant who replied – again in the affirmative.

Seven

Having given their details to the police, Kate and Jane went with Hetty to her dressing room to retrieve their coats. They then headed for the main door, although Jane hurried back for a dropped earring in Hetty's dressing room – which, luckily, she found.

For Kate, it wasn't clear how they might spend the rest of the day. They were meant to be enjoying rehearsals of *The Honeymoon* followed by a light dinner in the town and a return to the theatre for a performance of *The Admirable Crichton*.

Outside, Hetty left with Carole, who needed a lie down in bed.

Once they were out of earshot, Kate turned to her niece.

"Did you have something in mind earlier? Only, it's unlike you to drop earrings in people's dressing rooms."

"Possibly, Aunt. Now… what shall we do with the rest of the afternoon?"

Kate was undecided. The weather wasn't good and there wasn't anything she particularly wanted to see in the town. In the end, they settled for a return to the hotel for afternoon tea and a chance to do some reading.

Indeed, within the hour, they were seated comfortably in the quiet hotel lounge with its cheering fire and a welcoming view of spring daffodils and bluebells in the garden.

"Southshore has quite a few sea-going stories," said Jane. She was studying a slim volume on the locality's history. "Not all of them cheery."

"Storms wreaking havoc?"

Jane nodded and Kate shuddered.

"I don't think I'd like to be at sea during a storm, Jane."

"Me neither, Aunt."

"Mind you, I'm not all that keen about going to sea in *any* weather."

She put her magazine down. Idle chit-chat and the fashions in *Woman* magazine could wait.

"I can see you're not happy about something."

Jane sighed and put the slim historical guidebook down.

"Something doesn't add up."

"In what way?"

Jane kept her voice down so that the one other guest seated on the other side of the spacious room wouldn't hear.

"Hugh Calder, nearing his fortieth year, although we know he was nearly fifty. A leading actor, although perhaps getting a little old for the kind of roles he preferred. A collector of admirers, one of whom turned against him."

"There are some very odd people about, Jane."

"Yes, there are. So, who had an adverse opinion of Hugh. We could make a list."

Kate frowned.

"A list of people who disliked Hugh Calder…?"

"Yes, from raging hatred down to mild displeasure. First, we might consider who to place bottom of the 'We Dislike Hugh' list – perhaps someone who merely thought he was a show-off."

Kate's frown deepened.

"There might be quite a few candidates, Jane."

"Let's put Bill the caretaker-handyman bottom then."

"Why him?"

"Well, we have to start somewhere. I mean I know it would require a lot more information to be sure we've placed Bill correctly. For one thing, we'd have to know who else was vying for bottom spot on our list. Of course, with that kind of thinking, we would also end up asking…"

Jane paused and Kate slowly broke into a smile.

"Yes, Jane – we would also end up asking who'd be vying with the intruder for the top spot?"

"Precisely," said Jane. "Can anyone really say the intruder held the deepest grudge against Hugh? I mean… compared with who?"

"Alright, Jane, let's get serious then. Carole Adams looked up to Hugh. What if Angela thought there was more to it. It's possible she's glad to be rid of him. If *you and I* were the police, we'd follow that up."

"Unfortunately, we're not the police, Aunt."

"Ah, a visitor," said Kate, spying Hetty at the lounge door.

Jane gave a little wave and Hetty came over to join them.

"I was hoping I might find you here," she said.

She looked drained as she took a seat.

"How's Carole?" Jane asked.

"She's having a nap. Hopefully, she'll be alright."

"And what about you?" asked Kate.

"Oh… I'm not too bad. It's still a shock."

"You poor thing," said Jane.

"You should rest," said Kate. "I'd suggest an early night. If you can't sleep, try a comfortable fireside armchair and a dull book."

Hetty smiled.

"That sounds just the thing, Mrs Forbes."

"I know it's an awful business," said Jane, "but we must consider justice. You told the sergeant you hadn't noticed any strangers by the stage door recently."

Hetty seemed surprised.

"That's right… but… to be honest, none of us kept a close eye on Hugh's activities. He would have reacted badly to being spied on. If only we had, we might be able to give the police a description."

"Yes, of course," said Jane. "But here's something to consider – what if there's a different explanation for what happened."

Hetty looked confused, so Jane explained further.

"I'm sure the police are right to look for this intruder, but what if there's a chance Hugh's death was at someone else's hand?"

Hetty seemed to have it now, but equally seemed unwilling to accept it. Therefore, Jane pushed on.

"What if someone perceived Hugh and Carole's professional relationship as something more, and it pushed them into taking drastic action."

Hetty shrugged.

"It's possible, I suppose."

"It's just an idea," said Kate, "but if someone genuinely believed that Hugh and Carole were more than mere associates, then they might have harboured a grudge. Angela, for example."

Hetty sat upright.

"On that basis, you might as well round up Spencer for questioning."

"Ah yes, Spencer," said Kate. "Does he have plans for a future with Carole?"

"Yes, he does. At least, he did. I'm not sure anymore. For what it's worth, I prefer to believe that Carole was only receiving acting lessons from Hugh."

"Absolutely," said Kate. "Jane and I aren't suggesting anything else. It's just that… well…"

"Something doesn't add up," said Jane, completing her aunt's thought.

Hetty took a moment before responding.

"We all enjoy a little gossip from time to time. I do, myself. But this… it's so serious. I just don't want anything to do with gossip ever again."

"I don't blame you," said Kate. "It's rarely a force for good."

Hetty eyed them both.

"Are you looking into Hugh's death?"

"No, it's a police matter," said Kate. "We're just sitting by the fire speculating as to what might have happened. That's all."

"A parlour game then."

"Well…"

"Unfortunately, it's not a game," said Hetty. "Finding the intruder is all that matters now."

"You're right," said Jane. "It won't be easy without a description though."

"I agree with you there," said Hetty. "Southshore's a big place."

Kate could see Jane's disappointment. Hetty had failed to accept the possibility of competition for top spot on a list of suspects.

"Now, changing the subject," said Hetty, "a few of us are going to the Regency Dining Rooms later. It's one of our regular lunch venues but with the situation as it is… well, having dinner together seemed a good idea."

"It's a *very* good idea," said Kate. "Friends can be such a help during difficult times."

"I was hoping you both might join us."

"Oh," said Jane. "Are you sure we wouldn't get in the way?"

"Honestly, you'd be most welcome."

"Alright," said Kate. "We'll come along then."

Eight

Richard Harding fiddled with his fork for a while then put it down in its place on the table. With dinner yet to be served, he looked restless.

"First Friday off work in a while," he said in a joyless tone.

"Same here," said Spencer Wetherby. "It feels a little odd."

Kate nodded sympathetically to them both from across the table.

It was, in fact, two tables pushed together in the Regency Dining Rooms. Alongside Kate were Jane and Hetty. Sitting opposite were Carole, Richard and Spencer

"It was going to be a challenging summer at the Astoria," said Hetty. "It'll be even harder now."

"Perhaps not," said Richard.

"Now's not the time," said Hetty somewhat curtly.

"If you say so."

A curious Kate glanced at Richard, prompting him to explain.

"Hugh wouldn't appear in any production he didn't approve of, but he didn't give my new play any consideration whatsoever."

"Oh well…" said Kate, knowing that a playwright's work being rejected wasn't anything new.

Hetty softened.

"In fairness to Richard, it's a pretty good melodrama, which the audiences seem to go for."

"Well, I don't," said Spencer. "Anything but more melodrama."

"It's our bread and butter," Carole pointed out.

"Well, it shouldn't be."

"I'm not fixated on melodrama," said Richard. "My point is solely that the play should have been given a fair chance."

Kate decided to move things along.

"I suppose Angela and Neville weren't feeling up to dinner tonight. Quite understandable, of course. This whole business has been a shock for you all."

"Angela would sometimes be with us for lunch," said Hetty. She clearly realised the implications of her words and quickly added, "Mainly, she'd be with Hugh though."

Kate had come to understand that these actors would rise late in the morning, have a light breakfast then enjoy time to themselves. Lunch would be the day's main meal, followed by an hour or so of rest then a read through of upcoming work, then rehearsals, and a snack and some rest before that evening's performance.

"Neville would never have come," said Richard. "He rarely mixes with the rest of us. I'm sure the last time was Christmas."

"He takes lunch at the better restaurants," said Spencer. "Sometimes with an old friend or two. I don't see why he'd change it for an impromptu evening meal, especially after what's happened."

"What about Hugh?" asked Jane. "That is, when he wasn't having lunch with Angela?"

"He'd join Neville occasionally," said Richard.

"Hugh preferred Angela for company though," said Carole.

This assertion had Kate now wondering if Hugh's reputation for enjoying the company of admirers had in fact been a trivial thing – a courting of flattery and nothing more.

"Poor Hugh," said Spencer.

"Yes, poor dear Hugh," said Carole.

"This intruder," said Hetty. "The thought of it makes me shiver."

"Hopefully, the police will have some success," said Carole. "The killer can't hide forever."

"No, indeed," said Jane.

Kate noted that her niece had chosen not to reveal her feeling that something wasn't quite right.

"Perhaps Hugh was in part to blame," said Richard. "You can't give admirers a false intimation of your depth of feelings and expect to avoid a backlash."

"Murder though?" sighed Hetty.

"He didn't deserve it," said Carole. "I've said it before, and I'll say it again. Hugh was a changed man."

"Was he though?" asked Spencer. "I mean… can a leopard change its spots?"

"Please don't say that," said Carole. "Hugh was starting again with a new outlook."

"Really?"

"Yes, *really*. He wanted to be a mature leader. And he was certainly being genuine when he suggested he could help me improve my craft."

Glances were exchanged around the table and Kate decided she needed to get a grip. What *was* the truth? Hugh's past wasn't in doubt. But had he really changed?

She considered it further. What if he *had* changed. It wouldn't necessarily influence the attitude of those who encountered the previous incarnation of Hugh Calder. Was his change… his belated growing up, perhaps… even relevant to what happened?

Carole continued. "He felt I might be good enough for the West End or this new way of hearing a play on the radio."

"He was right about that," said Spencer. "Your future was always going to be rosy, regardless of Hugh Calder."

All stared at him, so he continued.

"Hugh upset someone enough to get himself killed. I'm merely suggesting it need have no bearing on Carole's future, that's all."

Carole looked a little awkward at the attention from Spencer.

"Let's hope the police get to the bottom of it," she said for the second time. "Hugh didn't deserve to die."

"Some people will do the worst of things when slighted," warned Richard. "Hopefully, the police will pick up on some mistake they've made and nab them."

"But why send anonymous poison pen letters?" said Jane.

"I don't follow you," said Richard.

"Sending letters such as those puts the intended victim on their guard. It might even draw in the police or a private detective. If a slighted admirer has decided on murder, why make the task more difficult than it need be?"

"Perhaps they only decided on murder in the last day or so," said Spencer.

"Then why bring another letter?" asked Jane.

Jane's point was met with silence, although Kate could see cogs turning in several heads.

"Perhaps they…" began Hetty, seemingly clutching for some kind of explanation, "…perhaps they had no plan to commit murder until they were on their way to the theatre."

"Then why leave home with a gun?" stated Jane quite bluntly.

"No matter," said Richard, happily eyeing a waitress bringing a plate of beef stew and dumplings towards him. "Scotland Yard's man will be here in the morning."

"Yes," said Kate. "I wonder what he'll make of it all?"

Nine

After a satisfying hotpot, Kate and Jane left the actors and headed out into the busy evening. Beneath a dark, cloudy sky, the central streets of the port town felt cold and impersonal. Despite the best efforts of the street lighting, it was no place for people to enjoy a stroll – more a place for sailors to roister from pub to pub.

Kate thought of her own hometown – smaller, quieter, more congenial.

"I was thinking of Sandham, Jane."

"I know what you mean, Aunt. Perhaps it's time we spent a few days there together…?"

Kate's heart swelled.

"That's a wonderful idea! I can picture it now – a lovely, quiet time together, enjoying the sea air with no drama whatsoever!"

"It sounds perfect."

At the end of the street, Jane indicated that they should turn left.

"Jane...? The hotel's the other way."

"I had a word with Hetty about where Neville Calder might be having dinner."

"I'm not sure we should bother him, Jane."

"I know, but a few questions might throw some light on something that might otherwise bother me for weeks to come."

Kate shrugged and joined her niece on this new and unexpected mission. Indeed, it wasn't long before they halted outside a quiet restaurant called the Albany.

"This is one of Neville's lunchtime haunts," said Jane. "I'll call you if he's inside."

Jane entered, leaving Kate to peer through the window. She could see her niece talking with a waiter. There didn't seem to be any sign of Neville Calder among those seated though.

Jane returned.

"He's not here, but they know him well and where else he eats."

He wasn't in the next restaurant either. Nor the one after it.

But then they tried the Royalty Chop House.

"Yes, he's in there," said Jane, peering through the window. "Ah... he's not alone."

Kate came alongside and squinted into the dim interior.

"Oh... it's Angela. Should we be surprised?"

"I'm not sure, Aunt."

"They're most likely sharing memories of a lost loved one – and they probably won't want us interrupting them."

Jane gave a little sigh.

"You're right – they won't. That said, someone murdered Hugh Calder in a cowardly attack. They shot him in the back."

Now it was Kate's turn to sigh.

"It's a fair point. Killers would have it easy if no one in mourning could be questioned. The thing is – it's surely the police who should be doing the questioning."

"Agreed, Aunt. But where are they?"

"Well, they're not here, obviously. I expect they're doing nothing until Scotland Yard's man turns up."

"By which time, the killer will be further out of reach."

Kate nibbled her lip.

"I suppose... put like that... sensibilities might occasionally need to take a back seat."

"I'll only question them if we're both in favour, Aunt."

Kate acknowledged the reality of being an amateur investigator. That done, she nodded and followed Jane inside.

A moment later, she felt a complete fraud in pretending to be surprised to see a puffy-eyed Angela and a washed-out Neville. Despite this, she joined Jane in taking a table next to them while offering sympathy.

Kate's discomfort then took on a physical quality when a cheery waiter handed her a menu and recommended the steak pie with mashed potatoes. With fresh memories of a hearty hotpot, she sent him away with a suggestion he try again in five minutes.

Of course, it didn't escape her that Neville and Angela at a table for two looked for all the world like a couple. It was a stretch though to see it as suspicious.

"At least Hugh was happy in life," Kate ventured.

"Yes, he was," said Neville. "Very much so."

"No, I don't think he was," said Angela. "His everyday demeanour was the same but there was a change in him. I think he saw life becoming less interesting."

Jane joined in. "According to Carole, Hugh was taking a mature approach to turning forty. Or was it fifty…"

Angela smiled wearily.

"With respect, Carole didn't know Hugh as well as I did."

"Of course."

"However… it's probably fair to say he couldn't see himself being the leading man at fifty and beyond – at least not in the way he'd want. If he had a fear, it might have been not wanting to be reduced to playing older men in supporting roles."

"Sorry to mention Carole again," said Jane, "but she seems certain that Hugh didn't have that fear… that he'd managed to overcome it."

Neville snorted.

"Who knows what tales he told that girl to win her over."

"It hardly matters now," said Kate, looking directly at Angela, "but all those admirers… it must have hurt you."

Angela stared back at Kate.

"You have to remember that Hugh in his younger days was a magnetic presence. People were drawn to him."

"Yourself included?"

"Yes." Angela dwelt on it for a moment. "Whether there was a change in him recently is all rather academic. One of his so-called admirers turned against him."

Neville sniffed.

"We'll have a detective from Scotland Yard here tomorrow. I'm sure we'll soon see some progress."

"Yes, of course," said Kate.

"Can I ask," Angela added, "you both seem interested in the investigation. I mean more than the average person. I'm wondering why."

"Oh, no reason," said Kate, rising to leave. "Sorry to have bothered you."

"Aren't you staying for your dinner?"

"Oh…" Kate had forgotten about that. "No, it's time Jane and I afforded you both some respect."

A few moments later, aunt and niece were strolling off towards their hotel. Kate wasn't happy though.

"Jane, I feel terrible about that."

"Me too."

"If Angela still had feelings for Hugh then she has a long road ahead of her. Adapting to a life alone isn't plain sailing."

"I know, Aunt – and I know you speak from experience. You must miss Uncle Henry terribly."

"I do."

"I… well, I just thought we might get somewhere. I'm not usually the insensitive type."

"I know you're not, Jane, but I'm thinking we should leave it to Scotland Yard."

"You're right. As you say, at some point tomorrow, the police will finally start looking into it properly."

They didn't walk much farther before Kate slowed to a halt.

"It really bothers you, doesn't it."

Jane came to a halt too.

"I hate treading on toes, Aunt, but yes, it does. It bothers me enormously."

Kate shrugged.

"There's nothing we can do, Jane. A good night's sleep is what we need. Tomorrow we'll board our trains home and put this behind us."

"I completely agree."

"You do?"

"Yes, a good night's sleep and a train home. Although…"

"Although…?"

"Before the sleep and the train, how about we take a proper look at the scene of the crime – without having any police or actors there."

"You're not serious?"

"I'm very serious."

"Jane… the Astoria is closed – and I doubt the constable at the main entrance will be keen to let us in, even if we do have tickets for tonight's performance."

"We wouldn't need to trouble the constable, Aunt."

Kate eyed her niece.

"Wouldn't we?"

Ten

With their coats wrapped tightly about them and their bags held close to their sides, Kate and Jane slowed as they neared the Astoria.

"Thankfully, not too busy a scene, Aunt."

"No," said Kate, still uncertain as to their next move.

A lone constable was stationed outside the main entrance, no doubt to deter any sightseers who might otherwise gather out of sheer curiosity. Inside, just a couple of the foyer wall lights were on, giving the empty interior an eerie glow.

"It's Little Alfred Street for us, Aunt Kate."

"I don't think the stage door will be open, Jane."

"No, it won't."

No sooner the police officer became occupied with a young man who seemed set on gaining admission to the building, aunt and niece slipped down the quiet side street.

Briefly, Kate nursed thoughts of breaking a shoulder trying to force the stage door open. As it was, Jane stopped to pick up a metal dustbin before continuing beyond the stage door with Kate following in confusion.

"Jane…?"

Just short of the high wall that brought Little Alfred Street to a dead end, Jane stopped on the right, by a tall wrought iron gate that protected the dank alley running across the back of the theatre.

"Right, Aunt. The alley runs across the rear of the building then around the other side. There's a gate there too, up at the top."

"Ah, the beer delivery entrance. But why are we here?"

"You see that farthest window…?"

"Yes?"

"That's Angela's dressing room. The one before it is Hetty's."

"What of it, Jane?"

"It isn't locked."

Kate squinted at it.

"How can you tell?"

"I left the latch off."

Kate's eyes widened.

"You left the… because you had a feeling something wasn't right?"

"Yes."

"So, we're definitely going inside then."

"There's a chance we might be able to learn something about the intruder's attack. For example, what difficulties they had to overcome."

Jane looked to the top of the street where a young couple were walking past. Once they had gone, she placed the dustbin in front of the gate and climbed over.

"Put the bin back and meet me at the stage door, Aunt."

Kate did as requested.

A minute or so later, she could hear the stage door bolts sliding back. Then the door opened.

"Welcome to the Astoria, Aunt."

Inside, Jane had turned a couple of lights on to illuminate the corridor leading to the dressing rooms. Despite this, the theatre's basement looked gloomier than ever.

"Just think, Jane, we could have been coming in through the main entrance with an expectant crowd."

"To watch Hugh Calder as Crichton. It's a loss."

Jane closed the door and bolted it shut.

"The killer's footprints have been scuffed quite a bit," she said. "Those I saw earlier weren't just a little wet; they were muddy enough to suggest a kind of woman's dress shoe with a heel. With what we've learned so far, I'm wondering if the killer wanted the police to notice them."

Kate peered downward. While muddy scuffs were still visible, the definition had been compromised by others traipsing about.

"It's not very clear, is it."

"Unfortunately, it was only after we learned of the letter left on Hugh's dressing table that I felt something wasn't right – by which time, we'd all trampled over the scene."

"That's not your fault, Jane. You weren't in possession of all the facts."

"True, but Richard and Hetty told us about the letters when we first arrived. In my mind, I filed it away under 'Trivial'…"

"So did I. Neither of us came to the Astoria expecting to encounter a murder."

Jane seemed to be thinking of something, leaving Kate to contemplate the faint whiff of damp once more.

"This place is definitely in need of maintenance."

"I thought you said it had character."

"Hmm… it also has floorboards that creak at night."

"I'm sure they creak all the time."

"And it's so dingy. Also, I'd say it has… an atmosphere. I'm sure you feel it too."

"It's an old building, Aunt Kate. That's all. Unless…"

Kate gazed at her niece.

"Unless what?"

"Well… apparently… the Astoria's haunted by a Victorian actor."

The thought chilled Kate to the bone.

"No…"

"A chap called Maxwell. He tripped on a rug and fell off the stage."

"No…" repeated Kate.

"Do you believe in ghosts, Aunt?"

"Not during the daytime, no. But at night I can easily be persuaded."

"It's only a legend. Hetty told me about it when we were setting up the visit."

"Well, I wish she hadn't."

"Apparently, Richard doesn't like that sort of thing. That's why nothing was said earlier."

"Well, I'm with Richard."

"Alright, let's forget about Victorian spectres for now."

Jane's gaze was on Hugh Calder's closed dressing room door.

A moment later, they were at the threshold.

"Jane? Um… are we sure they've removed Hugh?"

Jane frowned and pushed the door open.

"Yes, he's gone."

"Right… good."

Jane entered and looked around, although there weren't many places to investigate. Kate meanwhile remained at the door, not really sure how to assist.

Her niece eventually returned with a little shake of the head.

"There's not much to help us in there."

From where they stood, the pair beheld the possibilities that lay in either direction.

"Let's try the other dressing rooms," said Jane.

They did so – with Jane trying them all, including the empty ones. It wasn't long before she was dismissing a wasted effort and marching round to the far corridor. Here, she went as far as the stairs, which were a mirror image of those along the other corridor – a set of steps up to the stage and a short flight down to the sub-basement beneath it.

"One moment, Aunt."

Jane flicked a light switch and tried the sub-basement. She returned quickly.

"Nothing there," she uttered.

On this side of the building, there was no storage area, but the far end of the corridor terminated at a closed door.

"The beer cellar," said Jane.

They strolled up to it, to find it was, as expected, bolted shut from the other side.

"Just as well I'm not thirsty, Jane."

"Let's go back," said her niece.

"Righto," said Kate, beginning to feel just a little tired.

Heading back the way they had come, they passed the stairs and, turning the corner, the lesser dressing rooms again. They didn't stop though – this time continuing past the scene of the crime once more, past the stage door, and round to where the storage area was situated.

"I suppose Neville will inherit," said Kate. "That's not an accusation, by the by. Actually, isn't there a brother in New York."

"Yes," said Jane.

"I don't suppose there's much money to come. Then again, I don't suppose Angela married Hugh for his wealth. They're provincial theatre people. I'm sure they understand the realities."

Jane peered into the storage area and thought for a few moments. She then led them to the stairs leading up to the stage. Here, she flicked a wall switch, which lit some basic lights high above them.

As expected, the stage was set for the opening scene of *The Admirable Crichton.*

"Do you know," said Kate, admiring the drawing room laid out before them, "I've never thought of a theatre without its performers before. It's the strangest thing. Mind you, those chairs look comfy..."

"They certainly do," said Jane. "Now, how about we take a look in the office."

"Good idea," said Kate, forcing her gaze away from a sumptuous woven-fabric armchair with a plump cushion.

Eleven

Kate knew of only one way to the office – through the doors at the back of the stalls and across the foyer. Unfortunately, that route wasn't safe. If the constable stationed outside didn't spot them in the eerie light, any eager sightseer most definitely would.

"I noticed another door into the office," said Jane, clearly sensing Kate's concern. "It would make sense that staff could get about behind the scenes."

She was indicating that they should return down the short flight of steps.

A moment later, back in the corridor, they peered ahead to the front of the building where, in the dim light, it was just possible to make out another flight of steps.

They followed the corridor to its end, where they climbed the stairs to a door.

Jane opened it.

"Bingo."

While they dared not risk switching on the office lights, the streetlamp outside helped Jane peek into the three-drawer grey metal filing cabinet while Kate looked across the two wall-mounted shelves.

"Wouldn't it be handy if we found some old newspapers with words cut out, Jane."

"That would be quite decisive, Aunt. To be honest, anything that might throw light on events would be handy."

Kate tried the waste-paper bin by Neville's desk. If a cleaner usually came in at the end of the office day, it wouldn't have happened today. Nothing in the rubbish helped though.

Next she tried Hugh's desk – and then his bin. Here, among various scraps, she found a screwed-up paper ball.

"Anything, Aunt?" said Jane, glancing over as Kate straightened it out.

"It hardly qualifies as paperwork," said Kate, holding it up to the faint light. "It's just some jottings. Names and amounts of money, to be exact. Jack Morgan, one hundred pounds; Martin, eighty-five; Bradbury, ninety. Debts, Jane?"

"Could be. Hugh might have been in trouble."

"It certainly adds up to a tidy sum. It might also explain why so little is spent on maintenance."

"Yes, although…"

"Although what?"

Jane came over.

"Bradbury… I saw that name in the filing cabinet."

Jane went back and found the file again.

"No… nothing unusual. I think we've hit a dead end for now. Bradbury might be something for Scotland Yard's man to look into."

Kate raised an eyebrow.

"We can hardly send him a note explaining that we burgled the place."

"No…"

A few moments later, they left the office and headed back along the corridor the way they had come.

"Oh well," said Kate, "if I recall correctly, you did say we'd have an exciting time in Southshore."

Jane almost laughed.

"A promise is a promise, Aunt."

They squeezed hands.

For Kate, despite this being a grisly business, it was heart-warming to be spending time with her niece. It hadn't been easy over the years. When Jane lost her mother, Annette to Spanish Flu in 1919, the bond between Kate and Jane remained strong for a time. After all, Annette had been Kate's funny, talented, loving younger sister. However, Jane eventually went up to Somerville College, Oxford and, for a long time, circumstances largely kept them apart. That is, until the shocking business at Linton Hall.

"Let's think for a bit," said Jane.

"Good idea," said Kate. "Why don't we take the weight off our feet while we do so. I believe the correct term is 'Aunt and niece enter stage right'…"

Now Jane did laugh – as Kate led them up the stairs to the wings and onto the stage.

"This furniture is better than mine at home," said Kate. "I wouldn't mind a lamp like that… and look at this lovely rug."

They each took a seat – Kate choosing the armchair she'd spied earlier. It was timely too, as she'd begun to feel a slight discomfort at all the rushing around after dinner – something she usually avoided. Fortunately, she had just the thing in her handbag.

"Mint?" she said, offering a small paper bag to Jane.

"Just the thing, Aunt."

As they sucked their sweets, Kate listened to the silence. Being such a large space, the stillness was deep. She could almost feel it.

"It should have been a lovely day, Jane."

"Mmm…"

"Instead of which…"

A faint noise from somewhere had Kate catch her breath.

"Are you sure we're alone, Jane?"

"It could be a rat."

Kate swallowed.

"I'd rather see Maxwell, the deceased Victorian actor than a… you-know-what."

The sound of footwear on the side steps from the beer cellar corridor rendered further speculation unnecessary.

"Not a rat then," whispered Jane.

"And not Maxwell either," whispered Kate. "That probably means it's the killer."

The ladies eased back into their seats as a tall-ish figure looked set to enter stage left. The new arrival continued a few steps past the entry point though and went behind the scenery.

Jane whispered again.

"It's a man, Aunt Kate. A real one. Actually, I think it's someone we know."

They listened to the footsteps, which continued behind the scenery and came to a halt on the other side of the drawing room door.

For Kate, it was time to sound cheery and not at all scared as she called out to the hidden party.

"Come in."

Twelve

The door handle turned, the door opened, and the prowler entered in a measured manner. His face was indeed familiar to Kate.

"Inspector Ridley!" she gasped. "Do have a seat."

The detective – grey-haired, early forties, standing tall in a dark blue suit – gazed out at the empty auditorium for a moment then took an armchair beside the mocked-up fireplace.

"You remember me then," said the man from Scotland Yard.

"Of course we remember you," said Kate, trying to sound as convivial as possible. "We met at a previous murder."

"It's good to see you again, Inspector," said Jane.

"Hmm… I saw your names on the initial report. What on earth are you doing here? No… actually, I came in by the front door. A constable let me in. How did you two get in?"

"Well…" Kate was having trouble answering. "I feel I ought to offer you some tea, but the butler's taken the evening off."

Ridley fixed them with his gaze.

"Mrs Forbes, Lady Jane – why are you sneaking around an empty theatre at night? An empty theatre where someone was murdered earlier?"

"Um…" said Kate, still trying to think of something. "How did you get into that corridor?"

Ridley frowned. "I came through the stalls, stepped onto the stage and went down the side bit."

"The wings, Inspector," said Jane.

"Yes, well, I explored the corridor then returned to the stage to find a couple of uninvited house guests. Now give me one good reason not to throw you out."

Kate raised an eyebrow.

"I have a packet of mints?"

"Apart from that."

Kate rose and met the inspector midway across the stage, mints at the ready.

"We weren't expecting someone from Scotland Yard to get here before morning."

"Sorry to ruin your schedule," said Ridley, taking a mint., "but I arrived an hour ago. I thought it might be worth taking a look around while it's quiet."

"It really is the best way, isn't it," said Kate.

"I wasn't expecting to be disturbed by trespassers, Mrs Forbes."

"No, but now we're here, perhaps you should have this." She handed him the piece of paper from Hugh's wastepaper bin. "I found it in the office."

"Illegally searching the premises? I'm surprised at you, Mrs Forbes, what with your late husband having been a judge."

Kate thought of Henry for a moment.

"Inspector… a thousand apologies, but Jane had a feeling."

"More an itch," said Jane. "One I've yet to scratch."

Ridley popped the mint into his mouth as they retook their seats. He then cast an eye over the piece of paper.

"What is it?" he asked.

"We're not sure," said Jane, "but hang on to it."

Ridley slid it into an inside pocket.

"What was your opinion of Hugh Calder?" he asked.

"Well," said Kate, "more pertinent is the opinion he had of himself. He was a proud leading man who believed his quality would be enough to bring much-needed success."

"Not a shrinking wallflower then," said Ridley.

"No."

"Hmm… you've broken in. You must have had a good reason."

"We have a theory or two about members of the theatrical company," said Jane. "Nothing concrete though."

"I'm more interested in this intruder. Sergeant Halstead said there were wet footprints leading from the stage door to Hugh Calder's dressing room. Ergo, the killer was a crazed fanatic who came in from outside."

"I expect you've read the letters," said Jane.

"Yes," said Ridley, patting his jacket over the inside pocket to suggest he had them on him.

"Anything unusual?" asked Kate. "Apart from them being written by a crazed murderer."

"I can't talk about evidence, Mrs Forbes. I'm sure you understand."

"Of course."

Jane tilted her head slightly.

"Over the years, Hugh Calder invited many admirers backstage – usually ladies. I can see why you might think the killer is a disgruntled fanatic. I'd imagine the letters point you in that direction."

Ridley seemed to gauge Jane. Whatever his calculations, he relaxed a little.

"They're all anonymous and creepy," he said. "The last one was particularly disturbing. *Why do you still reject me… you'll regret it'* and so on."

"We're in agreement, Inspector," said Jane. "There's a dangerous person on the loose. I'm assuming the police have questioned the shopkeepers opposite the theatre."

"Yes, but no-one saw anyone leave by the side street. That said, I reckon it would have been fairly easy to miss them."

"From memory," said Jane, "the footprints leading to Hugh's dressing room were a kind of woman's dress shoe with the sort of thick heel that would be about two inches. It makes no sense."

"Go on…"

"What if things had gone wrong? Surely flat, sensible shoes are made for a planned getaway."

Ridley considered it for a moment.

"It's a fair point. An escaping killer might have to break into a trot at any moment."

"Also," said Jane, "the stride pattern was off."

"Alright," said Ridley. "I like your thinking on this. I'm not saying I agree, but I'm listening."

Thirteen

Kate, Jane and the inspector settled more fully into their comfortable seats. Indeed, Kate found herself looking for a footstool – although she dismissed the notion quickly, fearing that putting her feet up might lead to her dozing off. Jane meanwhile was very much awake.

"Why rule out the killer being a member of the company?"

"I won't rule anything out, Lady Jane. I might have to look for motives and opportunity though. Have you come up with anything in those directions?"

"Opportunity… I think Sergeant Halstead may have given you a list of everyone's whereabouts – as reported by themselves."

"Yes, it's in my pocket. I'm curious to know your thoughts though – without having me jog your memory."

"A test?" Kate protested.

"We're not working together, Mrs Forbes. I'm quite capable of reading a list and making assumptions. Anything from you must come *solely* from you."

"Spencer Wetherby was in the far corridor," said Jane. "The one you came to the stage by. He didn't see anyone. Or, if you prefer, nobody saw him."

Ridley took his notebook out and jotted something down.

"Go on."

"Angela Calder said she was in her dressing room, but didn't hear a gunshot."

"It's possible," Ridley acknowledged. "It wouldn't have been a loud bang. Who else?"

"Carole was in the back of the stalls and Neville Calder was in the office."

"Yes… I'm not sure how helpful any of this is."

"Jane and I were having a guided tour," said Kate.

"Yes, the sergeant made a note of it. Special guests…"

"Special guests with alibis in Hetty Bryce and Richard Harding. They were our guides."

"It's alright, Mrs Forbes. I'm not interrogating you. Hetty Bryce and Richard Harding were showing you around though?"

"A charming couple," said Kate. "We were in the upstairs bar area when we heard the commotion. It was closed at the time."

"Alright," said Ridley. "You've both had the opportunity to observe the company at work. Seeing as I've yet to meet any of them, is there anything worth me knowing?"

"Possibly," said Kate. "We bumped into Neville and Angela having dinner together earlier."

"When you say, 'bumped into' do you mean 'tracked down'…?"

"Um… yes, that might be a slightly more accurate way of putting it."

Ridley considered it.

"The brother and the wife. Consoling each other?"

Kate shrugged.

"I'm not suggesting they're having an affair – far from it. Although that would give them both a motive."

"A possible affair. I'll keep it in mind."

"Then there's Carole Adams," said Jane. "She's a member of the cast who was receiving acting tuition from Hugh."

"She's at least twenty years Hugh's junior," said Kate, "I can't help thinking her boyfriend, Spencer Wetherby thought there was more to it."

Ridley raised an eyebrow.

"Interesting."

"We're also wondering what Hugh's widow, Angela made of it."

"Oh," said Ridley, "you mean Spencer Wetherby *and* Angela Calder might have thought Hugh and Carole were having an affair. That might give Angela Calder a motive *without* her having an affair with the brother."

"Hugh had a track record of flings," said Kate.

"Carole insists Hugh had changed his ways though," said Jane. "It's a matter of deciding whether you believe her or not."

Ridley made a note in his book.

"So… we possibly have Hugh Calder as a man ruining two relationships: his own and that of Carole and Spencer. Or we have Neville as a man ending Hugh and Angela's relationship by moving in on his brother's wife. Or, as Carole insists, Hugh is innocent of all charges, and someone has failed to see it that way. I'd say I need to know if Hugh Calder was really helping Carole Adams with acting lessons or if she's hiding the fact that they were having an affair. It's certainly a tangled web, whichever way you look at it."

Kate wrinkled her nose.

"Have we been of help, Inspector?"

Ridley nodded.

"Yes, thank you. Be aware though – it's still possible there really is a frustrated admirer at large in the town. I can't overlook that."

"No, you mustn't overlook that," said Kate. "Of course, finding someone with the gun, or even the gun itself – that would help no end."

"That's a tricky one," said Ridley. "It's possible the intruder would have got rid of it. After all, if we do manage to track them down, the gun would nail them. Much better to get rid of it as soon as possible. Even while leaving the scene of the crime."

He thought for a moment.

"The report I got said the constable searched the route to the exit and the dustbins outside. No sign of a weapon, though."

"Ah well," said Kate. "It's early days."

Suddenly, Jane sat forward.

"Of course…"

Kate eyed her niece.

"What is it?"

Jane rose from her seat and headed off the stage.

"This way," she said.

Fourteen

Kate and Ridley followed Jane into the storage area.

"With a bit of luck…" she uttered, mainly to herself.

They watched as she began sifting through a multitude of props large and small, either on messily packed shelves or leaning against the wall.

"Bear with me…"

"What *are* you looking for?" Ridley exclaimed.

Jane held up a wooden duck painted yellow and green.

"Not this, for sure."

Kate wondered if to make a "she's quackers" joke but decided against it.

Jane sighed. "Perhaps I'm wrong."

To Kate's horror, her niece was now holding a human skull.

"I'm assuming that's not another murder victim," said Ridley.

"A ghoulish but necessary prop," said Jane.

"Shakespeare?" said Kate. "Alas, poor Yorick?"

"Well remembered, Aunt. Don't let me stop you."

"I've already stopped myself, Jane. I'm not even sure which play it's from."

"Ahem," said Ridley, clearing his throat. "Alas, poor Yorick! I knew him, Horatio. A fellow of infinite jest… um…" He shrugged. "Sorry, my Shakespeare's not what it might be."

"It's from *Hamlet*," said Jane. "The gravedigger finds it." She held up the skull. "Prince Hamlet realises this is all that remains of Yorick, the court jester. Yorick was a lively presence during Hamlet's childhood, one who would regularly have all those around the table laughing their heads off. Hamlet has to reconcile how such a noisy, abundant life can become nothing at all."

"A lesson for us all," said Kate. "Especially in the light of Hugh Calder's demise."

"Alas, poor Hugh," said Ridley, eyeing the skull.

A silence fell.

"What must it have been like watching theatre in Shakespeare's time," Kate wondered. "I think I would have enjoyed it."

Jane gave a little laugh.

"Aunt, in Shakespeare's time, you would have missed half the productions."

"Why?"

"Most of the crowd had to stand."

"Stand? As in not be seated?"

"And rain didn't stop the performance or the crowd getting wet."

"It would seem I haven't missed much at all then."

"Perhaps it's time you ladies returned to your hotel," said Ridley.

"Yes, of course," said Kate.

Jane moved a pile of books to put the skull down.

"Oh…" she uttered.

"What is it?" asked Ridley.

"It's not a spider, is it?" said Kate. "Real or pretend."

"No, it's these," said Jane.

She held up a pair of black patent leather ladies dress shoes with two-inch heels, taking care to avoid touching the outer surfaces.

"Muddy shoes…" mused Ridley.

Jane nodded.

"I believe it's the pair used to mimic an intruder's progress to the scene of the murder."

Ridley puffed out his cheeks.

"Well… you were right, Lady Jane. There was no flippin' intruder."

"It would appear not."

"It doesn't tell us who put them there though."

"On the contrary, it does," said Jane. "You just have to factor in the dustbins outside."

"The dustbins?" echoed Ridley, clearly puzzled.

Jane smiled with relief.

"Could I ask you to do something first thing tomorrow morning?"

"Yes, what is it?" asked Ridley.

"It's vital that you make some telephone calls."

Fifteen

Just after ten o'clock the following morning, Kate, Jane and Inspector Ridley were back in the props storage area. This time they were joined by Sergeant Halstead, Constable Shanks and all those who were in the building at the time of the murder. Namely, Angela Calder, Neville Calder, Carole Adams, Spencer Wetherby, Richard Harding, Hetty Bryce and Bill the caretaker-handyman.

The policemen, Neville Calder, Bill and Jane all stood, while chairs had been brought in for Kate, Angela, Carole and Hetty. As for Richard and Spencer – they sat on boxes.

Ridley took charge – his first task being to field questions about the purpose of them all being there.

"I've invited you here as it's where Lady Jane Scott made a significant find relating to the death of Hugh Calder. I'll explain more in a moment, but first there are a few questions that need answering."

Spencer ignored the guidance.

"I trust Lady Jane Scott isn't about to accuse me of anything."

Ridley eyeballed him.

"Please allow me to ask my questions, Mr Wetherby."

Angela sighed. "Sorry, but what did Lady Jane find here?"

Ridley nodded to the constable, who had a paper parcel with him. Unwrapping it, he presented a pair of black patent leather ladies dress shoes with dried mud on the soles and heels.

"What do shoes have to do with anything?" asked Spencer.

"I might also ask why Lady Jane was searching the building," said Angela.

"One thing at a time," Ridley insisted. "Miss Bryce, could you confirm that it was normal for yourself and Mr Harding to show guests around?"

"Yes," said Hetty. "Neville likes to have us sweet-talk potential investors. He was particularly excited to have Lady Jane coming to see us. He felt a large donation might be forthcoming."

"I see… and do you take a regular route when you show guests around?"

Hetty nodded. "Yes, we do."

"It's a form of entertainment to butter them up," said Richard. "Then Neville gets them in his office for coffee and pressures them into supporting the theatre."

Neville Calder gently cleared his throat.

"It's not a crime."

"No, it's not a crime," said Ridley. "It does however provide both Mr Harding and Miss Bryce with an alibi."

Kate smiled at Hetty.

"I don't understand," said Angela. "Why would they need an alibi when there's an armed killer out there somewhere?"

"This brings us to those *without* an alibi," said Ridley, ignoring Angela's question. "I wasn't here when the unfortunate event took place, but two people I trust were very much present. Mrs Forbes and Lady Jane Scott. I'd like to ask them to guide me a little here…"

Kate was confident of one thing – that her niece was the one to guide the inspector. She nodded to Jane.

Jane acknowledged her aunt's approval and took half a step forward.

"What about the intruder?" said Spencer. "As Angela pointed out – they're out there with a gun."

"Possibly," said Jane. "Then again, possibly not."

Spencer looked set to question this, but Jane pushed on.

"Aunt Kate and I saw Neville and Angela in a restaurant last night. If we're looking for motives, it would be easy to construe that the two of them are having an affair." She held up a hand to forestall protests from both parties. "It would also be easy to presume that they were consoling each other, a brother and a wife, following the terrible event that took place."

"That's all it was," insisted Neville.

"Neville's right," said Angela. "It was nothing more. We were both in shock. We still are."

Jane gave her a moment.

"And what of your husband? Did you believe he was having an affair with Carole Adams?"

Carole's face turned ashen.

"Angela wouldn't be the only one thinking it," said Neville.

"I don't know," said Angela. "That's the truth."

"We weren't," said Carole, finding her voice. "Absolutely not."

Ridley looked to Spencer.

"Mr Wetherby? What did you believe? Hugh Calder had a history of flirting. Did you think he was stealing your girlfriend?"

Spencer Wetherby composed himself.

"I… I trust Carole… implicitly. I'm sure it was nothing."

"Hugh was very much a changed man," said Carole. "He was soon to turn fifty. He didn't hide that from me. He told me his father died at fifty. He found that a sobering thought."

"He was just helping you with your acting then," Jane surmised.

"He said I had a good chance of getting to the West End. He also said I had a voice that would work well on the radio. The BBC are looking into the regular broadcast of plays, so…"

Kate wondered. Did Hugh really see her potential and only wish to help her achieve greater success?

"Why was it so secretive?" asked Jane.

Carole shrugged.

"Neville would have thrown me out had he thought I was looking to move on."

Jane seemed to accept this but then changed tack.

"Hugh was actively encouraging you to move on, wasn't he. There was an urgency to his guidance."

Carole gave it some thought.

"Yes… he did seem keen for me to improve at quite a rate. That's why it was so intense, I suppose."

"Which is why you spent so much time with him?" Jane asked.

"Yes."

"I can't think why you'd want to leave," said Spencer.

"Neither can I," said Neville. "This is a very fine company and a much loved theatre."

"I might be able to help you there," said Jane. "There was a particular reason for Hugh pushing Carole to improve fast."

"I'd like to hear it," huffed Spencer.

"Well, you shall," said Jane. "It's this – Hugh Calder believed in Carole to such a degree that he wanted to help her refine her talent before the Astoria Theatre closed its doors for good."

A sudden, noisy outburst erupted. Ridley had to raise his hands and shout.

"Quiet, please, quiet!"

Sixteen

Neville Calder was incandescent, although he did his best to withhold an actual outburst.

"May I remind everyone that a deranged prowler entered the theatre and murdered my brother. I have no idea why the police aren't doing more about it."

Jane took a steadying breath.

"We learned earlier that having Richard and Hetty acting as guides puts guests in a good frame of mind before sitting down with Neville Calder who seeks to gain their financial support."

Neville scoffed.

"I think we've already established that keeping this place going is *not* a crime."

"Absolutely," said Jane, "but it meant that Richard, Hetty, Aunt Kate and I were in the upstairs bar at the time of the attack."

"I'm not sure I understand you. Frankly, you haven't said a single thing that justifies this complete waste of everyone's time."

Neville followed this by glaring at Ridley.

Ridley ignored him.

"Let me help you," said Jane. "Perhaps if I mention the dustbins in Little Alfred Street, you'll agree that this isn't a waste of time."

"The dustbins…?" Neville seemed fit to burst.

"Two of them are situated on the route the intruder would have taken in getting away. I wondered if they might want to get rid of the murder weapon as soon as possible. After all, the gun is the primary link between the killer and the crime. Why risk holding on to it any longer than necessary?"

Neville Calder again looked to Ridley, who continued to ignore him.

"Let's imagine the intruder's plan," said Jane. "Hugh received a series of disturbing unsigned letters using words cut from a newspaper – the last letter asked why he was still rejecting the sender. This obsessive admirer seemed to know a lot about the routines of the theatre, which would have helped when they planned their enterprise. Certainly, they came in by the stage door and easily found Hugh in his dressing room. Now, over the years Hugh invited many admiring young ladies backstage…"

"Do we have to go through all this?" asked Angela.

"Fair point," said Spencer.

"Whatever the intruder's state of mind, they committed the deed as planned," said Jane. "Fortunately for them, they weren't spotted fleeing up Little Alfred Street, which would mean a fugitive on the loose. Of course, this isn't a small town. The likelihood would be our killer slipping away, out of reach of the law."

"I've always said we need more police," said Neville. "The intruder has got away with it."

"I don't think so," said Jane.

"How can you say that?" said Neville, staring hard at her.

Jane met his gaze.

"Because the killer didn't escape via Little Alfred Street."

Yet again, Neville looked to Ridley.

But Jane got the nod to continue.

"The intruder left muddy footprints that told us they were wearing a woman's dress shoe with a heel. But surely, a planned getaway means wearing sensible shoes, on the basis that things might go awry. That said, a killer walking down Little Alfred Street towards the stage door would have to step into a dirty puddle to get mud on the soles of the shoes, which doesn't make sense. Anyone wearing dress shoes would have avoided the puddles – it's not difficult to do. Also, the mud content of the footprints leading to Hugh's dressing room wasn't correctly distributed in that little should have been present by the time the killer got to Hugh's door. Also, the stride pattern was a little off, suggesting the shoes were held by hand rather than placed by foot."

Neville gave a dismissive laugh.

"This is nonsense."

"The killer knew everyone's whereabouts, including Hugh's. He was always last to the stage."

"Inspector, please…"

"Angela's is the farthest dressing room from Hugh's. On that side of the building, she would go around by the beer cellar corridor to climb up to the stage. We already know that Spencer was readying himself in that corridor too. As for Hetty and Richard, they were busy showing myself and my aunt around."

"This proves nothing."

"Doesn't your office have a door that opens onto Little Alfred Street? I ask that because the killer came down the slope alongside the building, dipped the shoes in a muddy puddle and came in by the stage door. Then it was a matter of making a few footprints and shooting Hugh. That done, the killer left the scene."

"None of this makes sense. I loved my brother."

Ridley stepped in.

"Perhaps I can throw some light on it," he said. "Lady Jane suggested I look through the theatre's files for details of contractors who've worked here in recent years."

The inspector had told Kate and Jane it would be better to tell the story with a few modifications and not reveal that a couple of amateurs had broken in.

"Why would she suggest that?" asked Neville.

"A hunch," said Ridley. "One worth looking into. That's why I disturbed a judge late last night to get a search warrant."

The inspector produced the documentation.

"I then took Mrs Forbes and Lady Jane along as observers and I found a short but interesting list in the office."

Kate continued to be wide-eyed. He'd obtained the search warrant *after* they left.

Ridley meanwhile produced the scrap of paper Kate had found.

"It was screwed up in the wastepaper bin by Hugh Calder's desk. Jack Morgan, one hundred pounds; Martin, eighty-five; Bradbury, ninety. I thought it might be a list of debts he owed, but Lady Jane said she had seen the name of Bradbury in a newspaper advertisement."

Jane had, of course, seen the name in a file. It was a building firm.

Ridley continued. "She suggested I refrain from adding the figures together to get a total debt, but to see them as something entirely different. With that in mind, I made some telephone calls earlier. Jack Morgan and Sons, the Martin Brothers, and John Bradbury are all firms of general builders – any type of work undertaken."

Jane addressed Neville.

"Your brother was looking forward to a successful future. Not as a theatre owner though."

Neville looked shocked.

"I honestly don't know what you're talking about."

"You do, Mr Calder. You learned of Hugh's plans a couple of weeks ago. That's when you began sending the letters."

Seventeen

"I've had enough of this," said Neville. He looked set to leave, but the constable stepped forward to dissuade him.

Jane waited for the theatre's director to look to her again.

"Your brother was getting a few rough quotes for refurbishment work on the quiet."

"*What* refurbishment work?"

"The alterations necessary to convert the Astoria into a moving picture cinema."

Neville gasped. He wasn't alone.

"You can't possibly make that assumption!"

"Oh, come on, Mr Calder, it's not a great leap once we have all the pieces. The Astoria was losing money to the local picture houses and yet Hugh expected packed houses here by the summer. This wasn't your brother being an over-optimistic actor. He was busy helping Carole to reach the next level in her career before the Astoria Theatre closed for good. Hugh, himself, wasn't bothered by that. He had no plans to become an older performer playing lesser roles. He was upbeat because he was planning for a different future. That's why he was getting initial, rough quotes from builders for the necessary conversion work."

Neville looked crestfallen.

"He never said a word about it to me."

"Mr Calder, you know plenty of people. You hear things. A whisper, perhaps, but you knew."

"No, never. This is the first I've heard of it. Hugh kept it to himself."

"Hugh would have told you," said Jane. "Otherwise, he wouldn't have been using the office telephone yesterday to get rough quotes for the necessary alterations. No doubt, he didn't tell you earlier because he wanted to delay the inevitable confrontation. Had he told you before the letters started arriving, he'd have suspected your involvement."

Neville shook his head. "The letters were from a fanatic."

"That's something we can agree on," said Jane. "Hetty told us you were expecting a challenging summer. You were planning to do everything you could to get through it. But Hugh was already arranging to fix things in a different way. You knew full well he was referring to packed houses watching moving pictures. That's why he insisted you stop taking money from visitors to support the theatre when it wasn't necessary."

Again, Neville shook his head and for a moment Jane came to a halt. But it wasn't Neville who took advantage of the pause.

"Hugh revealed his plans yesterday morning," said Angela, her voice cutting through the impasse.

All looked to her.

"About the cinema scheme?" Ridley asked.

"Yes, he said he was waiting on some rough quotes to guide him as to what kind of alterations he could afford. The next step would be to arrange for detailed estimates, which would mean builders coming here to measure up."

"Would Hugh have told Neville?"

"He did. The three of us were together in the office."

"And what time would this have been?"

"Before anyone else arrived. He'd asked to see us."

Ridley's gaze remained on Angela.

"Were you and Neville Calder working together against your husband?"

Angela's eyes widened.

"No, never! That's the truth!"

Jane turned to Neville.

"Your brother was about to convert the Astoria into a cinema. That must have cut you to the core. Hugh was about to turn fifty. His life as a dashing leading man was over. Your life as a theatre director though… you could go on for years to come doing what you love. Of course, if Hugh died, then the next brother would take ownership. You, in fact."

Neville shook his head, but Jane pushed on.

"Hugh was looking forward to owning a successful moving picture house. With him giving up acting, he'd have taken on a management role. What would your role have become in the new venture? Working at the projector?"

A stony-faced Neville remained silent, so Jane continued.

"Despite there never being an intruder fleeing by the stage door, the practicalities don't change. Being found in possession of crucial evidence would be a disaster. While no gun was thrown into the dustbin outside, it doesn't mean I was wrong. It was just a matter of working out the real killer's escape route. That would be from Hugh's dressing room to the office."

"That goes straight past this place," said Spencer.

"It does," said Jane. "And, as you know, it was here last night that we found the shoes."

Neville made a move towards a cabinet, perhaps a little too furtively.

Kate studied him, as did Ridley.

"Mr Calder?" prompted Jane.

Neville opened the cabinet door and put his hand into an urn. A look of terror struck him.

"Looking for this?" said Ridley.

The inspector was holding up a small-bore handgun.

"Sorry about that, Mr Calder," said Jane, "I should have mentioned that we also found the gun – in the urn."

Neville's shoulders slumped and he withdrew his hand. He turned slowly.

"Hugh and Angela weren't living together," he said, sounding beaten. "My brother was staying at a hotel."

Angela stared down at the floor. Neville seemed to look at her with pity. Carole meanwhile simply looked stunned. This was clearly news to her.

"Hugh saw it as an opportunity," continued Neville. "He and Angela have a telephone at their house, but now Hugh was living where he could make calls without being overheard. He also had a hotel reception desk to take messages. A couple of weeks ago, he made some calls to London regarding the cost of buying a moving picture projector."

"You overheard all this?" asked Ridley.

Kate was wondering too, but Neville Calder laughed bleakly.

"No… no… I didn't overhear it."

He let his hollow mirth die away before continuing.

"A keen young man in London made a telephone call to Hugh's hotel. Unfortunately, Hugh was here at the Astoria. Now, this keen young man had hopes of a fat commission, so he wasn't interested in leaving a message at the hotel."

"He called the theatre," Jane surmised.

"I was alone in the office when the phone rang. The young man asked for Mr Calder. Before I could clarify which Mr Calder he wanted, he started telling me of a great deal he had for me regarding… the contemptible item. The office door was open. Hugh was outside smoking a cigarette. At that moment, I knew my future was in jeopardy. Rather than confront my brother, I called him to take the phone and told him I had no idea what it was about. I made some excuse and left the office… but I listened at the door. Hugh insisted that this chap was never to telephone him and to simply send the particulars to the hotel."

"Did you tell Angela Calder any of this?" asked Ridley.

"No," said Angela. "He didn't."

"No, I didn't," confirmed Neville. "To be frank, I thought Angela might support Hugh. Loyalty and all that. You see they'd split up at least three times before. They always ended up back together though."

To Kate, Angela looked as if she would prefer to be anywhere but here.

"This was always about passion," said Jane. "The newspaper cutouts cited betrayal. They can be read as much from a rebuffed woman as they can a spurned theatre director."

"Passion…" exhaled Ridley. "In my experience, at the farthest extremes, it's always dangerous. Neville Calder, I'm arresting you for the murder of your brother, Hugh Calder…"

While the inspector completed the arrest, a wave of relief swept over Kate. A tough challenge in Southshore was over and a killer would face justice.

In a way, it struck her as poetic. Theatre director Neville Calder had created a fantasy of poison pen letters and muddy footprints to steer the police towards a fictional intruder. But in constructing the drama, the seasoned professional had failed to consider a critical factor – Lady Jane Scott re-writing the final act.

Eighteen

Three Weeks Later...

Kate Forbes was looking forward to the opening night of the Astoria company's production of G. K. Chesterton's *Magic* – a delightful comedy in which a Duke's conceited nephew tries to expose a magician's tricks but gets spooked by one that defies explanation.

Arriving at the theatre with Jane an hour before the curtain was due to go up, there was the matter of meeting some familiar faces again.

Indeed, Hetty and Richard were waiting for them in the foyer.

"Bang on time," said Richard. "Welcome back to the Astoria."

"We're so relieved you've got going again, and so quickly," said Kate.

"The show must go on," said Hetty. "Although not the one we were rehearsing – too many memories."

"Completely understandable," said Jane.

"We also have three new cast members," said Richard, "so it's something of a fresh start."

"Spencer left us for a job in Bristol," Hetty explained. "Carole is with the BBC in London."

"Oh, good for her," said Kate. "Let's hope it works out."

"Angela is staying, thankfully," said Richard. "We need her experience more than ever."

"Never underestimate experience," said Kate.

"It'll be a full house tonight," said Hetty. "All the tickets went in an hour."

"Publicity is publicity," Jane opined.

"Rotten but true," said Richard.

"We don't have long before we have to get changed," said Hetty, glancing at the clock on the wall. "This way…"

Kate and Jane followed the actors into the office, where Richard addressed a middle-aged man in a smart grey suit seated behind Neville's desk.

"Mr Calder, this is Mrs Forbes and her niece, Lady Jane Scott."

A beaming Mr Calder rose from his chair and came to shake hands.

"Stephen Calder, at your service," he said with a slight New York accent, no doubt picked up during his long years away from England. "I've heard all about your role in getting to the bottom of what happened here, and I thank you for it. It was a shocking day, but we'll try to move forward in the right spirit."

"Indeed," said Kate pondering the funeral of one brother and the trial of the other. "Hopefully, you'll find time for pleasant matters while you're here."

"I'm sure I will, Mrs Forbes."

"Your brother, Hugh… he had plans."

"So do I. It's my intention to open a cinema."

"Really?"

So much for him saving the theatre.

"Yep," Stephen confirmed. "I was at the premiere of *The Jazz Singer* in New York last October – the first time anyone has spoken and sang on the big screen. When Al Jolson said, "You ain't heard nothing yet!" the audience cheered, and I knew the silent movie era was over."

"What a remarkable experience," said Jane.

"Too right, Lady Jane. Right now, that movie is showing to record crowds across America and those silent cinemas are in a long line to get fitted for sound. *The Jazz Singer* will most definitely open in England, most likely later this year. The entertainment world is changing fast. We have to move with it or be left behind."

"Breathtaking times," said Kate, trying to be as forward-looking as possible. "So, this place will become a talking picture cinema…"

Stephen raised an eyebrow.

"Not the Astoria, no."

"No?"

"Oh, Mrs Forbes, this place is too old for the modern age. I'll help them restore it, of course, but my time will be spent looking for a site for a new building and overseeing its construction."

"Quite an undertaking!"

"It is. You see, I've seen a new style in architecture – *le style moderne* – white stucco frontage, angular decorative windows, chevron and zig-zag designs, interior chrome with white and silver décor…"

"That certainly sounds imaginative," said Kate.

"I've come home for good, Mrs Forbes – and I'm going to put entertainment in this part of the world onto a new footing."

"That's wonderful," said Jane. "May we both wish you the very best of luck with it."

"Yes, indeed," said Kate, "all the luck in the world."

"Thanks! Um… I have a large cheque here you donated, Lady Jane."

He proffered it to Jane, but she smiled.

"Put it towards the Astoria fund."

"Oh, that's very generous. Thank you."

Kate turned to a smiling Hetty and Richard.

"The Astoria goes on then," she said. "That's marvellous news."

"Yes, it's very exciting," said Hetty, "and with Richard as our new director."

"Congratulations!" chorused both Kate and Jane.

"A man with a very bright future," said Stephen.

"And what about you, Hetty?" asked Kate. "What's your ambition?"

"To stay on the stage and hopefully sing."

"Oh."

"Hetty has a fine voice," said Richard. "She *will* sing."

"Will you perform musical comedies then?" asked Kate, seeing that songs and skits were an established form of entertainment.

"Not musical comedies, no," said Richard. "Musical theatre."

This puzzled Kate.

"Gilbert and Sullivan?"

"No, I'm thinking of the more modern flavour. Stephen has told you about a talking picture cinema, but he also has a soft spot for the stage."

"Indeed, I do," said Stephen. "And when I asked Richard and Hetty if they enjoyed songs on the stage, I knew we could work together. Tell 'em, Hetty."

Hetty was by now bubbling with excitement.

"I have a theatre-mad friend in New York who wrote to me about *Show Boat*, a new musical by Jerome Kern and Oscar Hammerstein. It's the story of those who perform and work aboard the Cotton Blossom on the Mississippi River. She says there are songs such as "Ol' Man River" that I should set sail for New York just to hear. The audiences on Broadway are going wild for it."

"It's true," said Stephen. "I've seen it myself."

"And will you go to New York, Hetty?" asked an enthralled Kate.

"No need, Mrs Forbes. The London West End production opens next month at the Theatre Royal, Drury Lane!"

Kate and Jane laughed and gave all the encouragement they could offer. Things were moving forward for Hetty and Richard – and Stephen was no stick in the mud either.

"We'd better get going," said Hetty. "Richard and I need to get changed."

Kate watched them turn for the door and noted how they held hands before they'd left the office. It didn't take a great detective to work out which way that particular relationship was going.

"Aunt? Why don't I take you to the bar for a small sherry before the performance?"

"Good idea, Jane."

"I almost forgot," said Stephen. He was holding out two tickets. "Best seats in the house."

"Thank you very much," said both ladies.

"There's also a little party after the show," said Stephen. "The actors insisted on it."

"Did they?" said Kate.

Stephen broke into a smile.

"I'd be very grateful if you'd both come along as my guests."

"We'll be there!" said Kate.

"Definitely!" said Jane.

As they left the office and headed for the bar, a thought struck Kate Forbes. Would life continue to surprise her in the most unexpected ways?

She very much hoped so.

The End (Until Next Time...)

The Lady Jane and Mrs Forbes Mysteries

Thank you for reading this short novella.
We do hope you enjoyed it.

For details of all the full-length novels in the series,
simply pop over to the website.

www.churstonmysteries.com

Printed in Great Britain
by Amazon

61353442R00063